BINKY

LICENSE TO SCRATCH

KIDS CAN PRESS

To Malcolm and Neala, for always rooting for Binky

Kids Can Press acknowledges the financial support of the Government of Ontario, through the Ontario Media Development Corporation's Ontario Book Initiative; the Ontario Arts Council; the Canada Council for the Arts; and the Government of Canada, through the CBF, for our publishing activity.

Published in Canada by
Kids Can Press Ltd.
25 Dockside Drive
Toronto, ON M5A 0B5

Published in the U.S. by
Kids Can Press Ltd.
2250 Military Road
Tonawanda, NY 14150

www.kidscanpress.com

The artwork in this book was rendered in ink, watercolor, cat fur, bits of kitty litter, the occasional paw print, dog slobber and some biological matter we cannot name.
The text is set in Fontoon.

Edited by Karen Li and Yasemin Uçar
Designed by Julia Naimska
Series design by Karen Powers

The hardcover edition of this book is smyth sewn casebound.
The paperback edition of this book is limp sewn with a drawn-on cover.
Manufactured in Shen Zhen, Guang Dong, P.R. China, in 4/2013 by Printplus Limited.

CM 13 0 9 8 7 6 5 4 3 2 1
CM PA 13 0 9 8 7 6 5 4 3 2 1

Library and Archives Canada Cataloguing in Publication

Spires, Ashley, 1978–
Binky, license to scratch / written and illustrated by Ashley Spires.

(A Binky adventure)
ISBN 978-1-55453-963-5 (bound)   ISBN 978-1-55453-964-2 (pbk.)

I. Title. II. Series: Spires, Ashley, 1978–. Binky adventure.

PS8637.P57B545 2013   jC813'.6   C2012-908580-4

Kids Can Press is a Corus™ Entertainment company

NO ANIMALS WERE HARMED IN THE MAKING OF THIS BOOK. A CAT HAD SOME ROUTINE BLOODWORK DONE AND A DOG WAS SUBJECTED TO SOME FOUL-TASTING LEFTOVERS, BUT THAT WAS THE EXTENT OF IT.

3

SUITCASES!

THEIR HUMANS ARE GOING AWAY!

urrr

WITHOUT THEM!

THEY RECEIVE AN S.O.S. FROM GRACIE. HER HUMANS ARE PACKING, TOO!

5

THEIR HUMANS ARE GOING INTO **DEEP SPACE** UNPROTECTED.

WHAT IF THE ALIENS ATTACK?

WHAT IF THEIR HUMANS DON'T MAKE IT BACK TO THE SPACE STATION?

WHO WILL GIVE BINKY AND GORDIE THEIR MEALS?

AT LEAST THE SPACE STATION WILL BE SAFE WITH THE FORCE FIELD ON ...

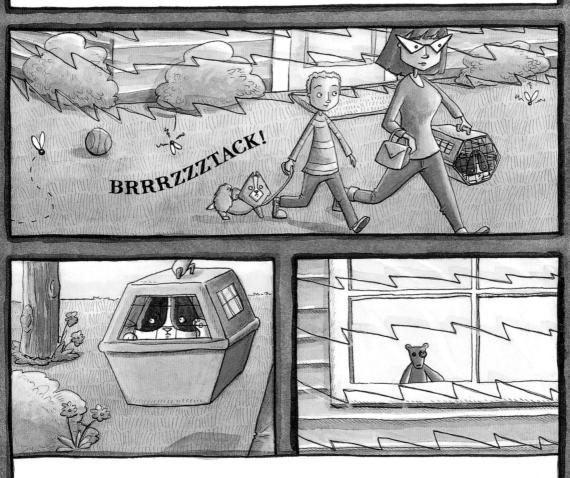

AND HIS COPILOT, TED, IN CHARGE.

WITH BINKY AND GRACIE TRAPPED IN PORTABLE SPACE PODS ...

GORDIE HAS TO ACT AS THEIR EYES.

HIS REPORTS ARE LESS DETAILED THAN THEY'D LIKE.

WHY DO THEY HAVE TO STAY **HERE?**

WHERE THEY POKE AND PROD AND TAKE YOUR TEMPERATURE?

splark

Bye-bye, guys! We'll be back in a few days. See you soon!

HOW COULD THEY LEAVE THEM IN SUCH A PRISON?

NOW WHAT IS HE SUPPOSED TO DO?

WHO KNEW BEING HELD CAPTIVE WAS SO BORING?

IT'S AN **EARTHQUAKE!** THE WHOLE BUILDING IS COMING DOWN!

IF HE COULD JUST GET AWAY ...

HEY!

THEN HE COULD ...

kerthunk

MAKE A BREAK FOR IT!

zoom

WUMP!

CRASH!

25

GRACIE! IS SHE ESCAPING, TOO?

Enjoy your playtime, kitties!

THAT MAY NOT HAVE BEEN THE ESCAPE HE HAD IN MIND ...

BUT AT LEAST HE FOUND GRACIE ...

AND TOGETHER, THEY CAN MAKE A PLAN TO GET OUT OF HERE.

WITH BOTH BINKY AND GRACIE LOCKED UP ...

THEIR BEST CHANCE OF ESCAPE IS GORDIE.

HE'S THE ONLY ONE WHO'S SEEN ENOUGH OF THE BUILDING ...

TO FIGURE A WAY OUT.

THEY WILL HAVE TO GET A MESSAGE TO HIM SOMEHOW.

WITH ANY LUCK, GORDON HASN'T COME BACK YET.

IT WORKED!

THE VENTS ARE THEIR BEST CHANCE FOR ESCAPE.

BUT HOW WILL THEY BREATHE IN **OUTER SPACE?**

PROTECTIVE SPACE GEAR!

click click click

WELL, WHAT ARE THEY WAITING FOR?

hmm ...

tlink

tlippa

brong

THAT WAS EASY. THE SCREWS WERE ALREADY LOOSENED.

MAYBE BINKY SHOULD HAVE TAKEN THE LEAD.

OF COURSE! A SECRET LAB BELOW THE VET ...

IS PERFECT FOR A SCIENTIST.

IT HAS ALL THE SUPPLIES ...

THAT SHE NEEDS FOR HER RESEARCH.

TO KEEP HER LAB A SECRET, TUFFY MUST SILENCE THE SPY.

WHAT THE HAIRBALL IS *THAT*?!?

IT'S NOT AN ALIEN.

IT'S NOT A CAT.

AND IT'S **NOT** PRETTY.

IT'S PROFESSOR TUFFY'S GREATEST ACCOMPLISHMENT!
AN ALIEN/FELINE HYBRID SHE CALLS ... THE FELIEN!

OR IAN FOR SHORT.

HE IS DESIGNED TO INFILTRATE AND HELP OVERTAKE ANY SPACE STATION!

Hi, kitty!

bzzzzzzzzzzz

Yipes!

BUT WHAT ABOUT HER OATH TO — ?

TUFFY DOESN'T CARE ABOUT PROTECTING HUMANS!

HER HUMANS DIDN'T PROTECT *HER*.

YEARS AGO, SHE HAD HER OWN HUMANS ...

HER OWN SPACE STATION ...

tinker blik

AND A BRIGHT FUTURE WITH P.U.R.S.T.

BUT THEN ONE DAY, HER HUMANS STARTED PACKING.

plunk

pitta patta

THEY PACKED UP EVERYTHING BUT HER.

SHE WAITED AND WAITED ...

BUT THEY NEVER CAME BACK.

pat
pat

HER HEART WAS SO BROKEN THAT SHE SURRENDERED TO THE ALIENS AND JOINED THEIR CAUSE.

ALIENS WORK AGAINST HUMANS, AND TUFFY WAS READY TO DO THE SAME.

THE ALIENS BROUGHT HER TO THIS SECRET LAB ...

AND SET HER TO WORK ON THE ULTIMATE WEAPON.

NOT ONLY HAS LIVING UNDER THE VET GIVEN HER ACCESS TO TECHNOLOGY ...

BUT IT HAS ALSO ALLOWED HER TO LEARN FROM THE VETERINARY DOCTOR.

PROFESSOR TUFFY HAS WATCHED THE DOCTOR FROM AFAR ...

WHILE SHE SAVED THE LIVES OF HUNDREDS OF CATS.

SHE'S DONE HER BEST TO STAY OUT OF SIGHT ...

vlink

Kitty?

BUT THE DOCTOR SPOTTED TUFFY ONCE OUT OF THE CORNER OF HER EYE.

THE ALIENS HAVE WHAT THEY WANTED. THEY DON'T NEED HER ANYMORE.

MEOOOR?!?

HOW COULD THIS HAPPEN? TUFFY HAS BEEN BETRAYED AGAIN!

POW!

CRUNCH!

AFTER ALL THAT EXCITEMENT ...

BINKY DOESN'T MIND RETURNING TO THE BOREDOM OF HIS CAGE.

WHO KNEW GOING ON VACATION WAS SO STRESSFUL?

SUDDENLY, BINKY HAS AN AWFUL THOUGHT.

TUFFY'S HUMANS NEVER CAME BACK FOR HER.

WHAT IF *THEIR* HUMANS DON'T COME BACK?

WHAT IF THEY'VE BEEN ...

ABANDONED!